The DREAM QUILT

by Celeste Ryan   illustrations by Mary Haverfield

WaterBrook
PRESS

Especially for

August, 2000

Michael, on the
3rd anniversary of his
baptism.

With love from

Aunt Maryanne &
Uncle Dave

Sometimes Michael had bad dreams.

He would wake up crying.
Mother would come to pray with him
and hold him until the bad feeling passed.

One morning Mother said,

"When I was little, I had scary dreams too.

Granny Rose would pray with me

and cover me up with my special quilt.

It made me feel so warm and safe."

"May I have a special quilt?"

Michael asked.

Mother went to her old cedar chest.

"Here's mine," she said.

"Would you like to sleep with it tonight

and play the game Granny Rose and I
used to play?"
"Sure!" said Michael.

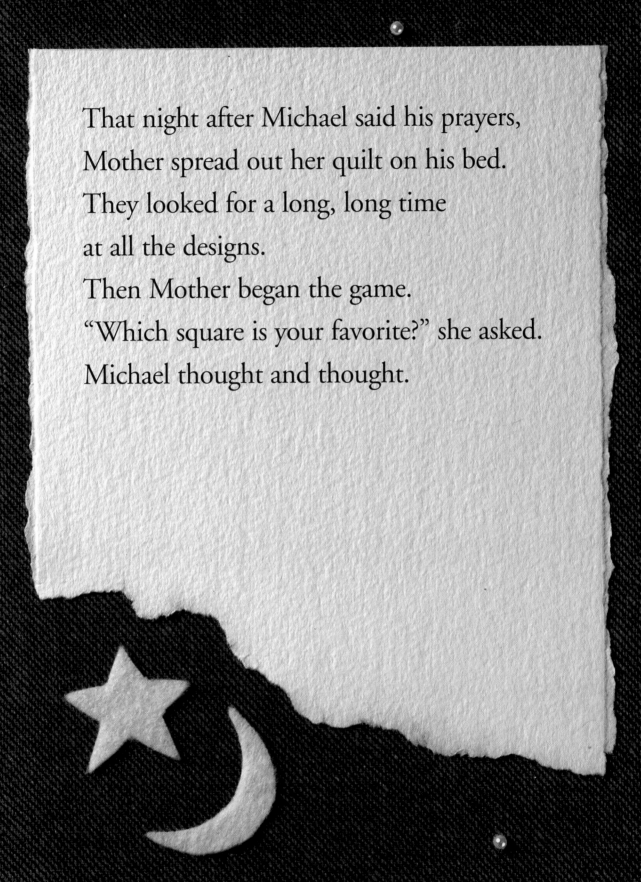

That night after Michael said his prayers,

Mother spread out her quilt on his bed.

They looked for a long, long time

at all the designs.

Then Mother began the game.

"Which square is your favorite?" she asked.

Michael thought and thought.

"This blue one," he answered.
"I like the ocean."

SPECIAL DELIVERY

AIR MAIL

Mother tucked the quilt
under Michael's chin and said,
"Now pretend you're a letter,
and this quilt is your envelope.
I'm sealing you up
to send you off to dreamland."

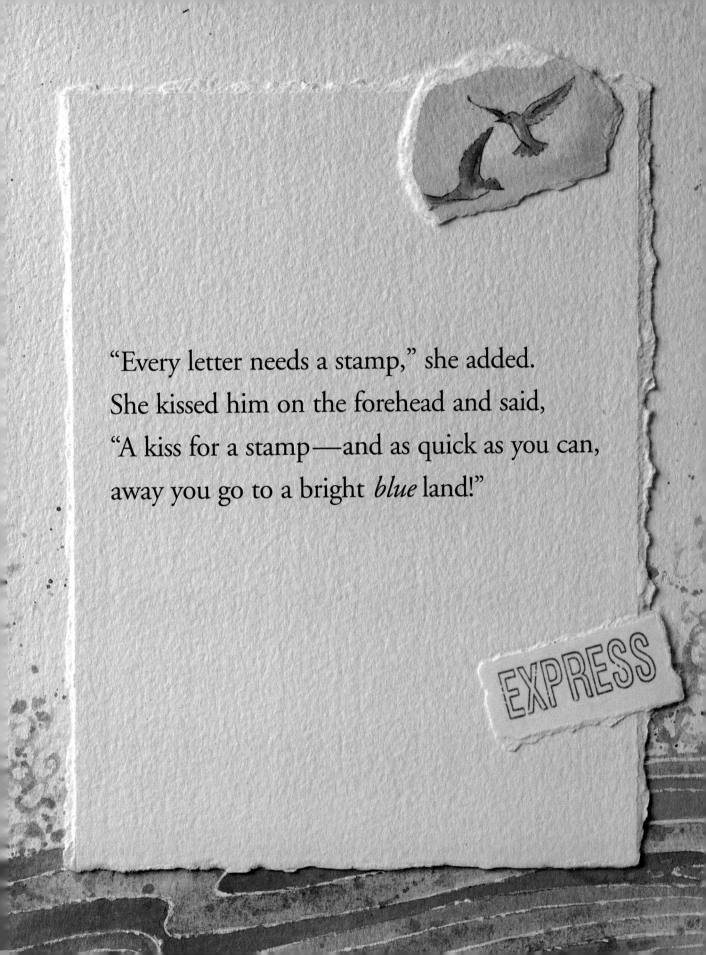

"Every letter needs a stamp," she added.
She kissed him on the forehead and said,
"A kiss for a stamp—and as quick as you can,
away you go to a bright *blue* land!"

That night Michael had blue dreams.

The next night Michael told his mother,
"I like this yellow square, too."

After his prayers, Mother tucked him
into the quilt envelope and kissed him.
"A kiss for a stamp—and as quick as you can,
away you go to a bright *yellow* land!"

That night was a yellow dream night.

The next night, while he was praying,
Michael kept noticing
a red square on the quilt.

When he was tucked in safe, his mother said,
"A kiss for a stamp—and as quick as you can,
away you go to a bright *red* land!"

That night Michael dreamed
wonderful red dreams.

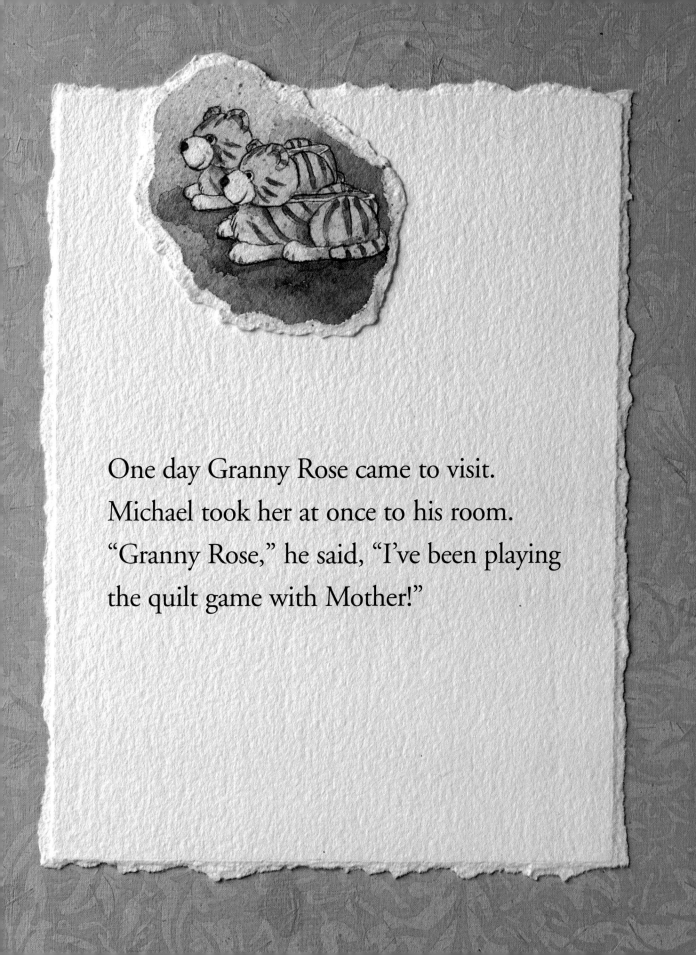

One day Granny Rose came to visit.
Michael took her at once to his room.
"Granny Rose," he said, "I've been playing
the quilt game with Mother!"

But Granny Rose looked worried.
"The old quilt is tearing a little,"
she said.
"Some of the squares are quite loose."
She turned to Michael's mother.
"I'll take it home and repair it for you,
then I'll send it back as soon as I can."

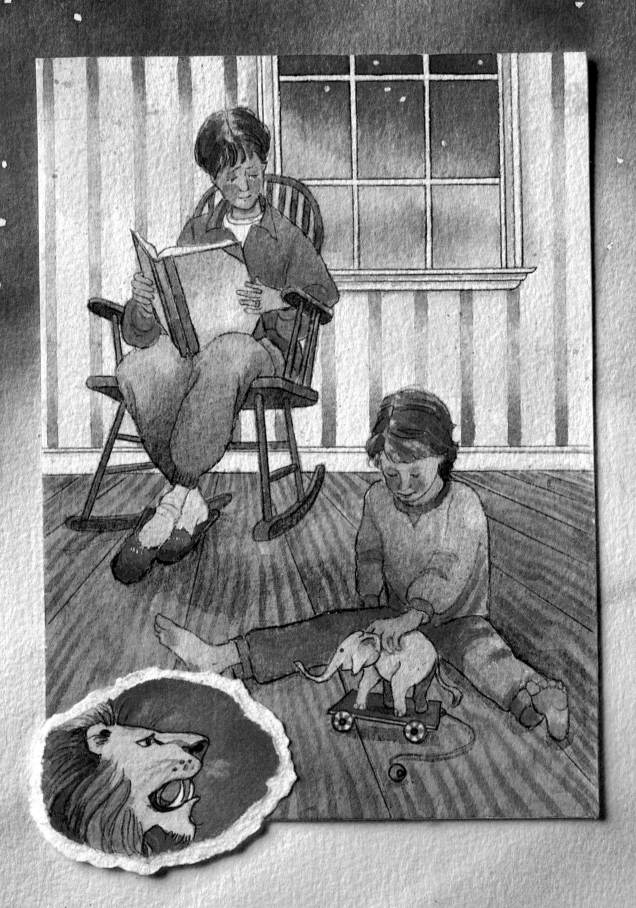

That night Michael said to his mother,
"I wonder if those old bad dreams
will come back?"

Mother held Michael close. Then she said,
"Remember how God saved Noah in the ark,
and all the animals, too?
Then God sent a rainbow to help us know
that He will always love us
with a strong, mighty love.

"A quilt cannot really protect you—but *God* can!
Because God is strong and God is loving."

At bedtime she pulled Michael's old blanket
up to his chin, sealed him up, and said,
"A kiss for a stamp—and as quick as you can,
away you go to a *rainbow* land!"

That night Michael had
wonderful rainbow dreams.

And the next night, too.

And the next night, too!

Granny Rose soon brought
back the special quilt,
but even when Michael
didn't play the quilt game,
he almost never had bad dreams again.

And every night he said to God,
"Thank You for Your strong and mighty love
that makes me feel warm and safe!"

"You, O God, are strong.

And You, O Lord, are loving."

PSALM 62:11-12

THE DREAM QUILT
PUBLISHED BY WATERBROOK PRESS
5446 North Academy Boulevard, Suite 200
Colorado Springs, Colorado 80918
A division of Random House, Inc.

Scripture taken from the *Holy Bible, New International Version®*.
NIV®. Copyright © 1973, 1978, 1984 by International Bible
Society. Used by permission of Zondervan Publishing House.
All rights reserved.

ISBN 1-57856-223-6

Library of Congress Cataloging-in-Publication Data
Ryan, Celeste.
        The dream quilt / by Celeste Ryan ; illustrations by Mary
Haverfield.
            p.   cm.
        Summary: A mother helps her son get over his bad dreams using her
old quilt and faith that God will always protect him.
        ISBN 1-57856-223-6
        [1. Dreams fiction.   2. Mother and child Fiction.   3. God Fiction.
4. Quilts Fiction.].   I. Haverfield, Mary, ill.   II. Title.
PZ7.R9485Dr   1999
[E]—dc21   99-24665
                                                   CIP

Printed in the United States of America
1999—First Edition

10 9 8 7 6 5 4 3 2 1